Over in

JOHN LANGSTAFF

the MEADOW

With pictures by

FEODOR ROJANKOVSKY

VOYAGER BOOKS • HARCOURT, INC

ORLANDO AUSTIN NEW YORK SAN DIEGO TORONTO LONDON

Also by John Langstaff and Feodor Rojankovsky
FROG WENT A-COURTIN'
(Caldecott Award Winner, 1956)

JIM ALONG, JOSIE
A Collection of Folk Songs and Singing Games for Young Children
by John Langstaff, with Nancy Langstaff

For information about permission to reproduce selections from this book,
please write Permissions, Houghton Mifflin Harcourt Publishing Company,
215 Park Avenue South, NY, NY 10003.

Voyager Books is a registered trademark of Harcourt, Inc.

Library of Congress Catalog Card Number: 57-8587

Printed in China by RR Donnelley, China

ISBN 0-15-258854-X   ISBN 0-15-670500-1 pb

SCP   30 29
4500579582

Printed in China

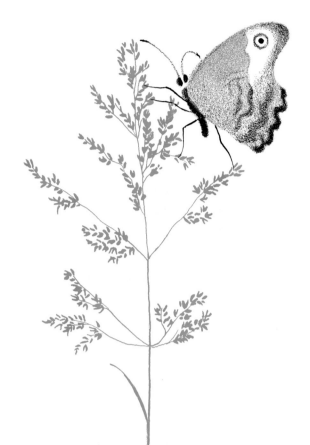

For Deborah
who loved this song about baby animals
so much when she was two that she sang
it wherever she went

Next time you go for a walk in the country, see if *you* can find some of the animals in this meadow. Walk gently and watch closely . . . they are sure to be there!

J. L.

Over in the meadow

in the sand in the sun

Lived an old mother turtle and her little turtle one.
"Dig," said the mother,

"I dig," said the one;
So he dug and was glad in the sand in the sun.

Over in the meadow where the tall grass grew
Lived an old mother red fox and her little foxes two.

"Run," said the mother,
"We run," said the two;
So they ran and were glad where the tall grass grew.

Over in the meadow in a nest in a tree
Lived an old mother robin and her little birdies three.
"Sing," said the mother,
"We sing," said the three;

So they sang and were glad in their nest in the tree.

Over in the meadow by a tall sycamore
Lived an old mother chipmunk and her little chipmunks four.
"Play," said the mother,
"We play," said the four;
So they played and were glad by the tall sycamore.

Over in the meadow in a new little hive
Lived an old mother queen bee and her honeybees five.
"Hum," said the mother,
"We hum," said the five;
So they hummed and were glad in their new little hive.

Over in the meadow in a dam built of sticks
Lived an old mother beaver and her little beavers six.
"Build," said the mother,

"We build," said the six;
So they built and were glad in the dam built of sticks.

Over in the meadow in the green wet bogs
Lived an old mother froggie and her seven polliwogs.
"Swim," said the mother,

"We swim," said the 'wogs;
So they swam and were glad in the green wet bogs.

Over in the meadow as the day grew late
Lived an old mother owl and her little owls eight.
"Wink," said the mother,
"We wink," said the eight;
So they winked and were glad as the day grew late.

Over in the meadow in a web on the pine
Lived an old mother spider and her little spiders nine.

"Spin," said the mother,
"We spin," said the nine;
So they spun and were glad in their web on the pine.

Over in the meadow in a warm little den
Lived an old mother rabbit and her little bunnies ten.
"Hop," said the mother,

"We hop," said the ten;
So they hopped and were glad in their warm little den.

OVER IN THE MEADOW

Tune set by Marshall Woodbridge

Over in the mead-ow in the sand in the sun Lived an old moth-er tur-tle and her lit-tle tur-tle one. "Dig," said the moth-er, "I dig," said the one; So he dug and was glad in the sand in the sun.

Ped. . . . . . . *

Over in the meadow where the tall grass grew
   Lived an old mother red fox and her little foxes two.
"Run," said the mother,
"We run," said the two;
   So they ran and were glad where the tall grass grew.

Over in the meadow in a nest in a tree
   Lived an old mother robin and her little birdies three.
"Sing," said the mother,
"We sing," said the three;
   So they sang and were glad in their nest in the tree.

Over in the meadow by a tall sycamore
   Lived an old mother chipmunk and her little chipmunks four.
"Play," said the mother,
"We play," said the four;
   So they played and were glad by the tall sycamore.

Over in the meadow in a new little hive
   Lived an old mother queen bee and her honeybees five.
"Hum," said the mother,
"We hum," said the five;
   So they hummed and were glad in their new little hive.

Over in the meadow in a dam built of sticks
   Lived an old mother beaver and her little beavers six.
"Build," said the mother,
"We build," said the six;
   So they built and were glad in the dam built of sticks.

Over in the meadow in the green wet bogs
   Lived an old mother froggie and her seven polliwogs.
"Swim," said the mother,
"We swim," said the 'wogs;
   So they swam and were glad in the green wet bogs.

Over in the meadow as the day grew late
   Lived an old mother owl and her little owls eight.
"Wink," said the mother,
"We wink," said the eight;
   So they winked and were glad as the day grew late.

Over in the meadow in a web on the pine
   Lived an old mother spider and her little spiders nine.
"Spin," said the mother,
"We spin," said the nine;
   So they spun and were glad in their web on the pine.

Over in the meadow in a warm little den
   Lived an old mother rabbit and her little bunnies ten.
"Hop," said the mother,
"We hop," said the ten;
   So they hopped and were glad in their warm little den.